Skywriting with Worm

Me as a baby

Found this cool meteorite

For Cory and Jessica
—D.C.

For my beautiful niece, Maddy. I love you.
—H.B.

Diary of a Fly   Text copyright © 2007 by Doreen Cronin
Illustrations copyright © 2007 by Harry Bliss   Printed
in the United States of America.   All rights reserved.
www.harpercollinschildrens.com   Library of Congress
Cataloging-in-Publication Data   Cronin, Doreen.   Diary of a
Fly / by Doreen Cronin ; pictures by Harry Bliss. — 1st ed.
p. cm.   Summary: A young fly realizes, day by day, that there
is a lot to learn about mastering flight school and getting along
with 327 brothers and sisters, and she discovers that heroes
come in all shapes and sizes.   ISBN-10: 0-06-000156-8 (trade bdg.) ISBN-10:
0-06-000157-7 (lib. bdg.) — ISBN-13:978-0-06-000156-9 (trade
bdg.) — ISBN-13:978-0-06-000157-6 (lib. bdg.) ISBN-10:
(lib. bdg.)   [1. Flies—Fiction.   2. Diaries—Fiction.]
Bliss, Harry, date, ill. II. Title.   PZ7.C88135Dfl
2007   2006006064   [E]—dc22   CIP   AC
by Neil Swaab   1 2 3 4 5 6 7 8 9 10   Typography
First Edition

DIARY OF A FLY

By Doreen Cronin

Pictures by Harry Bliss

JOANNA COTLER BOOKS
An Imprint of HarperCollinsPublishers

JUNE 7

Tomorrow is the first day of school. I'm so nervous. What if I'm the only one who eats regurgitated food?

JUNE 8

Great news! Everyone eats regurgitated food!

JUNE 10

Things they teach you in flight class:
We are the most accomplished
fliers on the planet.
Our average speed is 4.5 mph.
Leap backward when taking off.

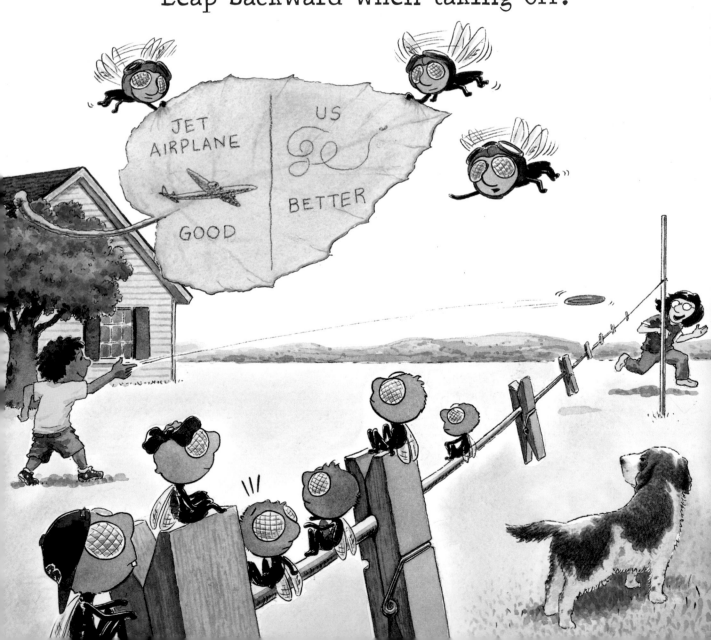

Things they should teach you in flight class:
Always have a flight plan.

ZIP

WHOOSH

JUNE 12

My parents left us with a babysitter last night. When they got home, eighty-seven of us were stuck to a strip of flypaper.

Mom says we were a lot easier to watch before we grew heads.

JUNE 14

Today we practiced landing on moving targets.

I am standing on her head right now.

My school picture came out terrible.

Mom says next time I better have all
my eyes looking in the same direction.

JUNE 17

My first science assignment
is to use my five senses
to observe something creepy.
I chose a first grader.

JUNE 18

Worm and Spider came over today.
We used a magnifying glass to take
a really good look at ourselves.

YOGURT

ICE CREAM

ROOT BEER

I'm making an "All About Me" book
for my mom:

I told her we could put half of them
in the garage to save space.

I'm having a time-out
in the garage right now.

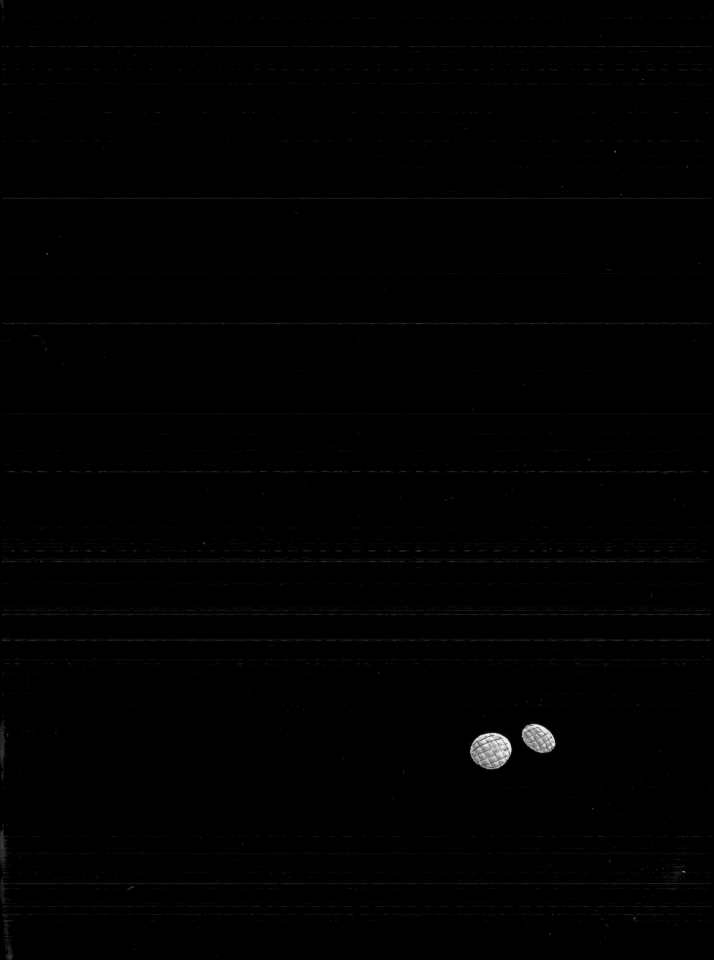

JULY 14

Spider's grandfather is so smart. He taught me flies were a very important part of the food chain. Very cool.

You're very important!

JULY 15

Worm sat me down and explained
the food chain.

That is so not cool.

JULY 16

The babysitter came back last night.
She brought a frog.

When Mom and Dad got home,
we were all exactly where we were
when they left.

JULY 21

Why I would make a good superhero:

I have the most
powerful flight
muscles on
the planet.

I can land upside down.

I can see in all
directions at once.

Spider said, "Superheroes bend steel with their bare hands. You eat horse manure with your feet."

I never thought about it that way.

JULY 22

Today I learned that flies beat their wings 200 times per second.

= 200!

ERASE KING™

ALL-PURPOSE ERASER

No wonder I keep falling asleep in math.

JULY 23

I visited my aunt Rita today.
She's been trapped on the wrong
side of a screen for a week.

My word . . .
how you've
grown, dear.

AUGUST 1

I just know I would make an excellent
superhero:
   I have 4,000 lenses in each eye.
   I can walk on walls.
   I can change directions in flight
      faster than the blink of a human eye.

Spider said, "Superheroes save the world from outer-space villains. Your brain is the size of a sesame seed."

I never thought about it that way.

AUGUST 2

Today I told Worm and Spider that I could never be a superhero like I wanted.

Worm looked me right in the eyes and said, "The world needs all kinds of heroes."

Spider said, "I never thought about it that way."

Neither did I.

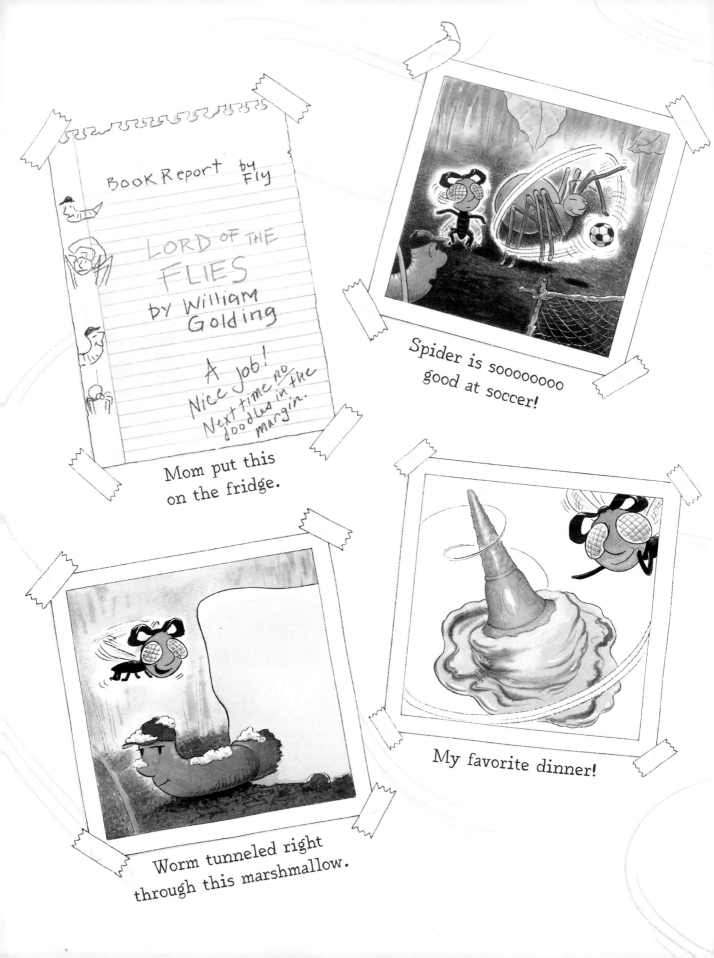

Book Report by Fly

LORD OF THE FLIES
by William Golding

A Job!
Nice time no
Next doodles in the
margin.

Mom put this
on the fridge.

Spider is soooooooo
good at soccer!

Worm tunneled right
through this marshmallow.

My favorite dinner!